Dulcie Dando,
Soccer Star

Dulcie Dando, Soccer Star

SUE STOPS
illustrated by DEBI GLIORI

Henry Holt and Company • New York

First American edition
Published by Henry Holt and Company, Inc.,
115 West 18th Street, New York, New York 10011.
Published simultaneously in Canada by Fitzhenry & Whiteside Ltd.,
91 Granton Drive, Richmond Hill, Ontario L4B 2N5.
Originally published in Great Britain by André Deutsch Limited, London.

Library of Congress Cataloging-in-Publication Data
Stops, Sue.
    Dulcie Dando, soccer star / Sue Stops;
illustrated by Debi Gliori.
    Summary: Dulcie, a talented soccer player, proves that
girls are just as capable as boys when she's given the
chance to play on the school team during a big game.
    ISBN 0-8050-2413-1
    [1. Soccer—Fiction.   2. Sex role—Fiction.]   I. Gliori, Debi,
ill.   II. Title.
PZ7.S8836Du   1992   [E]—dc20   92-2259

Printed in Great Britain.

10 9 8 7 6 5 4 3 2 1

Dulcie Dando was last in a long line of daring ladies.

Her mother rode around on a motorcycle with Dulcie on the back. Her granny could dive from the highest diving board.

Her great-granny raced on bicycles and her
great-great-granny rode horses.

Although Dulcie Dando was extremely proud of all her
relatives, she wanted to be different. The thing she was
best at was…soccer! She was brilliant!

The girls at St. Mathilda's School thought that she was the greatest. The boys weren't so sure.

One day Mr. Newman put up a notice announcing the
team for the annual soccer match against their deadly
rivals, St. Jude's. Only boys had been selected. Dulcie
Dando's name wasn't there.

"Why isn't Dulcie on the team?" asked Suzannah Price, Dulcie's best friend. "She's better than all the boys put together!"

"Well," said Mr. Newman. "Ours has always been an all-boys team. But Dulcie is a fantastic soccer player, so I don't see why we can't include her. We'd better think again."

He consulted the boys.

"We don't want her on the team," said Tom. "She'll get in the way, get hurt and start crying. I can't stand girls who cry, and anyway—she's got soft shins!"

Mr. Newman was stumped. He knew the boys were being unfair, but he didn't want to upset them before the big match. "I know what we'll do," he suggested. "We'll make Dulcie the first substitute."

Dulcie was furious. She was so upset that she felt angry spurts of water shoot into her eyes. "I'll show them...." she muttered to herself, as she kicked an old lemonade can all the way home. "I'll show them!"

"Dulcie's in a bad mood this evening," remarked her mother to her father. "I think I'll take her for a spin on the motorcycle to see if I can cheer her up." But Dulcie didn't want to go.

Instead she took a soccer ball out into the backyard and practiced heading and saving and dribbling and passing to the cat.

Game Day dawned. The girls weren't exactly overjoyed about the event, because Dulcie wasn't playing, but they decided to go as fans. Dulcie dragged along behind the rest.

The boys went to the locker room where Mr. Newman gave each player a new uniform. They liked the smell of the new material and stroked the shiny new shorts. Then they all got changed. All, that is, except Billy Thompson.

Billy was struggling. The shirt wouldn't go over his head, the shorts wouldn't go over his bottom, and the socks hardly reached his ankles. "This uniform's too small for me," he told Mr. Newman.

"Let's see the label, Billy," Mr. Newman replied, fiddling around at the back of the shirt. "Oh—brother! It looks as if they've sent one that's too small. It says 'S' on it. You'll have to wear your old uniform."

"But I didn't bring it," wailed Billy.

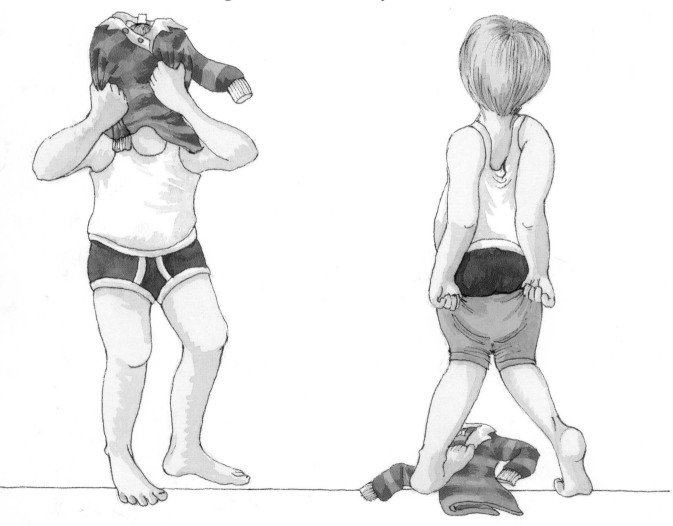

"Maybe someone's got a spare uniform,"
said Mr. Newman hopefully.
But no one did.
"Well, I'm not playing, anyway!" said Billy.
"I'd look stupid if I wasn't dressed
like the rest of the team!"
He ran from the locker room
before anyone could see
that he was crying.

But someone saw him! Dulcie Dando had climbed onto a wall outside the locker room to get a better view of the game, and when she saw Billy's streaky cheeks, her lightning-quick, computerlike brain told her she was needed. She went to the door and knocked.

Mr. Newman answered.
"Got a problem, sir?" she asked.
"Well, Dulcie, we have, as a matter of fact. It's a question of size. They've sent the wrong…good heavens! An amazing thought has just crossed my mind. It might fit you!"

"Bet your life it will!" said Dulcie.
She breathed in very hard, and just managed to squeeze into the tiny uniform. Then she ran out with the rest of the team. The first substitute indeed!

The girls cheered on Dulcie Dando, who had, of course, worn her soccer cleats—just in case.

The girls danced with delight.
The boys were mad.

The whistle blew. St. Jude's center forward got the ball, but was intercepted by Dulcie Dando who quickly dribbled toward the goal. Whizzing by four players, she deftly and generously passed to Alex Smith who shot the ball into the back of the net.

The girls cheered.

The boys clapped politely.

Then St. Jude's got a goal. The score remained one–one until there were just two minutes left to go. Dulcie Dando got the ball and went to give it an almighty kick when—TWANG—the too-tight buttons on her shorts popped off and her shorts fell to the ground. All she was left wearing was her pink underwear!

The girls gasped. The boys fell apart laughing. The boys from St. Jude's just stood and stared.

They were so surprised they completely forgot that Dulcie Dando still had the ball. She, not caring one bit about the others, dribbled it toward the goal—WHAM—straight past the dumbfounded goalie. The whistle blew. 2–1 to St. Mathilda's! The girls cheered! The boys cheered! Even St. Jude's cheered. Dulcie Dando's mom tooted the horn on her motorcycle like mad.

Dulcie heard it and, not caring at all about being in her underwear, ran across the field to her mother. Then, to the sound of even greater cheering, she leapt on the back of the motorcycle, put on her helmet, and away they roared into the setting sun.